GRANDMA PANDA'S CHINA STORYBOOK

Legends, Traditions and Fun

Written and Illustrated by
Mingmei Yip

TUTTLE Publishing

Tokyo | Rutland, Vermont | Singapore

Contents

To Geoffrey, who makes the whole world beautiful!

Preface

My book **Chinese Children's Favorite Stories** retold thirteen of the most popular Chinese traditional tales. For this new book, I have created the loving and knowledgeable Grandma Panda, who teaches her little grandchildren about Chinese culture through storytelling, action or both. Because Pandas are China's most beloved animals, it is my hope that these cute creatures will act as ambassadors and introduce children of all cultures to the fascination of China's thousands-of-years old traditions.

I chose eight interesting Chinese legends and traditions for Grandma Panda to share with her eager grandchildren —and with children all over the world: dim sum (snacks); the writing system; painting dragons; kung fu; kite—flying; opera masks; making music; and the story of the beloved woman warrior, Mulan.

The Chinese people express their hopes for their children by saying, "Children are the pillars of our country's future." Now that the world is shrinking, we all need to know something about how others live. I hope that children will enjoy these tales, and at the same time learn something about life in one of the world's oldest cultures.

Enjoy!

Yum Yum, We Love Dim Sum!

It's summer at last! Little pandas Baobao and Lingling are excited because summer is when they visit Grandma Panda, who cooks them tasty food and tells them wonderful stories. Any story you can name, Grandma can tell it. Baobao and Lingling love to learn as much as they love to eat. Each summer they learn so much and eat so well at Grandma Panda's that they can't wait to visit again!

"Grandma, we're here!" they shout as they jump off the bus and scurry on chubby feet toward their grandmother. Grandma Panda takes her grandchildren in her arms and kisses them on their fluffy heads.

"Grandma, I'm hungry!" Baobao cries.

"Me too!" Lingling joins in.

"All right, all right. I know you two are always hungry." Grandma Panda smiles at her two little treasures.

"Grandma, can we have noodle soup with lots of bamboo shoots, and egg fuyong with lots of roast pork, and...." Baobao begs.

"But today I'm not going to cook," Grandma replies.

"But what are we going to eat?" the children cry.

"Be patient, kids," Grandma Panda says. "We're all going to a tea house for dim sum. How's that?"

Brother and sister burst out laughing. "Wah! We love dim sum!"

It's Sunday, and the Lucky Tea House is filled with happy customers. After settling down at a round table, Baobao and Lingling stare at the steaming plates on carts that waiters and waitresses are rolling between the tables.

Grandma Panda says, "Now, Baobao and Lingling, pick what you want. Just don't stuff yourselves till your tummies look like balloons!"

Brother and sister reach out to grab from the passing carts:

Flat rice noodles with roast pork, Shrimp dumplings nestling in a bamboo steamer, Spare ribs dripping with sauce, Crispy spring rolls...

In no time the table is covered with little plates, and all that can be heard are the sounds of clicking chopsticks and the slurping of soup.

"Hmmm...yum yum dim sum!" exclaims Baobao, his mouth full of food.

"And yummy crispy!" A big smile blossoms on Lingling's face as she munches a crunchy spring roll.

Soon all the food is gone and the empty plates shine like bright mirrors. Baobao and Lingling rub their tummies and sigh with satisfaction.

"Grandma, please tell us a story!" says Lingling.

"A story about dim sum!" adds Baobao.

"All right, then," Grandma says. "But first, tell me, do you know what *dim sum* means?"

The children shake their heads.

"It means 'heart toucher,'" Grandma smiles.

Baobao is puzzled. "But it only fills my stomach."

"Yes," Grandma says, "but after your stomach is filled, your heart feels happy. That's how dim sum touches your heart."

"Wah! We want our hearts to be touched all the time!" Lingling cries.

Dim sum is made up of lots of different little dishes served together. In earlier times, people would enjoy just a few of these dishes, along with some tea, as a little "touch" or snack.

Grandma laughs. "As long as you're with me, you'll always have plenty of dim sum. Now listen—this is the story of how it was invented."

Once a long, long time ago, General Caocao and his army fought hard and won many battles. To celebrate his soldiers' loyalty and fearlessness, Caocao declared there would be a big feast.

The general ordered delicious dishes from every soldier's hometown to be sent to the battlefield.

The soldiers felt pleased beyond words.

"Wah, this pork dumpling tastes exactly like what my wife fixes back home!" one exclaimed.

Another one laughed as if the sun were shining right over his head. "This beef noodle is definitely my grandma's cooking!"

General Caocao smiled warmly at his men. "Please soldiers, eat more! If this pleases you, from now on every day I'll offer you a little of my heart!"

And so these little plates of comforting food became "Dim Sum." For *dim* means "a little," and *sum* means "heart."

勤有功戲無益

Sun

Ancient Chinese

Modern Chinese

日

Moon

Ancient Chinese

Modern Chinese

月

Grandma Panda Teaches Us Chinese Writing

That night Baobao and Lingling sleep soundly, dreaming of endless plates of steaming dim sum. The next morning, they are full of energy and ready to play. But Grandma Panda has other ideas. She is busy fussing with writing tools—brushes, ink, ink stone, and big, clean sheets of rice paper.

"Grandma, what's that for?" the children ask.

"Today is a good day to stay home and study Chinese," Grandma replies.

"But we want to go out and play!" the children cry.

Grandma Panda smiles. "Sorry, kids, you're Chinese so you have to learn Chinese. After that, you can have all the dim sum you want. Deal?"

Thinking of all the delicious mouth-watering dishes, the children agree with a loud "Yes!"

Soon, all three are sitting at the table, each with a brush, a small plate of ink, and a large sheet of rice paper.

"Baobao and Lingling, don't slouch," Grandma says. "Also, hold your brush straight in your hand. The great Chinese calligrapher Yan Zhenqing said that only when your brush is straight will your mind be straight. You want your minds to be crooked?"

"No!" brother and sister cry.

"Good. Now watch how I paint lines and dots to form characters. Once, most of the characters looked like little pictures. See, these were the characters for moon, rain, water and mountain. Now what do you think this means?" Grandma paints the sun and moon together.

The two little pandas are puzzled.

"It means bright—Because the sun and the moon shine in the sky."

"Yes, we get it!" the children exclaim.

The two little ones have a lot of fun painting Chinese characters. When they finish, Baobao plants a kiss on his grandma's cheek. "We love Chinese calligraphy! Thank you, teacher Grandma!"

Grandma Panda laughs and pats their heads. "Good. Don't thank me—thank Cang Jie, who invented Chinese writing. Listen. I'm going to tell you his story."

Cang Jie was born in ancient China. What made him different from everyone else was that he had four eyes!

As a child, Cang Jie was very curious. With his four eyes, he studied plants, flowers, insects, birds, and animals. Cang Jie spent his nights looking up at heaven and his days observing all things on earth. Staring up at the moon and stars, he asked himself: Why is the moon sometimes round like a melon, while other times it is curved like a fingernail? Why do the stars keep winking at me all night long?

Looking down at the earth he saw mountains, rivers, and trees, heard thunder and felt rain and wind. He saw that everything had its own nature: the mountains tall and solid; the rivers soft and flowing; the rain noisy as it watered the earth; the wind powerful, able to blow things far, far away. Cang Jie also studied the different footprints on the mud, trying to figure out what animals had left their marks there. He learned the different tracks of snakes, lizards, turtles, birds, boars, tigers, and elephants. Chang Jie learned so much, he knew he'd never be able to keep it all in his head, so to help him remember, he invented writing. Alas, Cang Jie wrote on mud, so his characters were long ago washed away. But we still have some very old Chinese that was written on turtle shells or cow bones, telling us how the Chinese used to live.

The Chinese began to write over 3000 years ago, at first on animal bones and bamboo, later with a brush on paper. Chinese writing is not only useful, it can be very beautiful. Beautiful handwriting is called calligraphy. The best calligraphers were honored all over China and their writings are shown in museums throughout the world.

Dotting the Dragon's Eyes

Baobao and Lingling love writing the characters so much that they are happy to sit and practice. But after a while, the two little treasures are tired and beg Grandma to tell them another story. Grandma gives them each a bowl of red bean soup. As they eat, Grandma begins her story in her comforting voice.

Once upon a time there lived a painter called Zhang Sengyao. Zhang was much admired in his hometown for his wonderful skill in painting flowers and animals, especially dragons. He could make these mythical beasts look alive: scales glittering, long whiskers swaying, tails wagging. But, strangely, none of Zhang's dragons had eyes.

While Zhang's admirers praised his dragons, they were puzzled by their sightlessness. "Master Zhang, why don't you put in the eyes?"

Zhang's answer was always, "If I paint the eyes, the dragon will come alive!"

One day when Zhang was traveling in the province of Jingling he spotted the famous Peace and Joy Temple. Noticing its bare wall, he exclaimed, "Perfect for painting!" And so he took out his brush and began to paint.

Soon a large group gathered to watch. Under the graceful movements of Zhang's brush, the beast began to appear on the wall. Next, Zhang splashed color on its twisting body.

Amazed at Zhang's creation, everyone cupped their mouths and held their noses, fearing that the sound of their breathing would break the painter's concentration and destroy his magic.

As Zhang stepped back to regard his masterpiece, the audience began to chatter.

"This is not a man's work, but heaven's!"

"Tell me, are my eyes blurred, or is the dragon really moving?"

Zhang continued wielding his brush in all four directions. Soon there were not one but two huge dragons on the temple wall, stretching their limbs and swishing their tails. As usual, to the audience's great disappointment, neither had eyes.

One young woman gathered up courage and asked, "Master, why don't you paint the eyes?"

Zhang smiled. He knew that the people of Jingling hadn't heard of him and didn't know his style. "Because once I put in the eyes, the dragon will come alive! I paint to please, not to scare."

"Hahaha, coming alive, what nonsense!" one man laughed.

Next to him, a stout man grinned ear to ear. "Master, I am fearless, and never saw a dragon coming to life, so please open the dragons' eyes!"

Zhang decided it was time to show his true colors. He took a deep breath then, with two swift strokes of his brush and a loud shout, he dotted in one dragon's eyes.

As he finished, dark clouds rolled across the sky, lightning flashed and rain began to pour. To the astonishment of the crowd, the dragon began to twist into kungfu poses: an eagle about to attack, a mantis snatching a cicada, a general riding his wild horse. In no time, it leapt off the wall and, with a deafening roar, flew away!

Amazed, the audience could only gasp.

When the din died down the people saw that only the sightless dragon remained on the wall. No one, not even the fearless man, dared to ask Zhang to dot its eyes.

Since then, Zhang's fame spread wide and far. Later, people would use this story of "Dotting the Dragon's Eyes" to teach a lesson: paying attention to small details can make all the difference.

The dragon, a mythical animal imagined to fly through the clouds, is one of China's most famous symbols. For the Chinese, dragons are not evil, but represent strength, nobility and good luck. The Chinese love the mystical creature so much that they call themselves the "Dragon's Descendants." In China, dragons are everywhere—paintings, folk tales, songs, clothes, bowls, plates, good luck charms.

The Story of Mulan, the Brave Woman Warrior

After hearing about the great Zhang Sengyao, Baobao and Lingling work even harder at their calligraphy, paying attention to details. To reward them for their hard work, Grandma Panda tells them one of their favorite stories—the tale of Mulan the Woman Warrior.

Once upon a time, in the war-torn north, a young girl named Mulan lived with her parents and her younger brother. Ever since she was little, her father had taught her martial arts. Every day, Mulan practiced hand fighting, sword fighting, horse riding, and archery, never realizing that one day she would put all these skills to use.

In the north, Chinese had suffered from the invasion of the Xiong Nu—the Barbarians. Every year men—young or old, strong or weak—were called to fight these ferocious invaders.

At last, one day, Mulan's family received the emperor's order.

"What are we going to do?" her father cried. "I am too old to fight but I may not refuse!"

Mulan's mother sobbed to her daughter. "Your poor father has been sick for years! If he joins the army, he'll collapse on the road even before he has a chance to fight!"

Alarmed at the idea of her frail father being taken away to the battlefield, Mulan had an idea. "Don't worry," she said. "I'll go in Father's place."

Her parents looked as shocked as if their only daughter had suddenly turned into a man in front of their eyes.

But that was exactly Mulan's plan. She would disguise herself as a man and go to fight.

17

Having no other choice, her parents agreed, even though Mulan had just been betrothed to Han Shiqi, a young man who had also been called to fight.

For twelve long years, the two fought side by side without Han ever knowing that his brave comrade was in fact his beautiful fiancee!

During these difficult years, Mulan fought and won many battles. Once, after she discovered that the Barbarians intended a sneak attack, she drummed up a clever plan. The oldest, weakest soldiers were sent to the front to fight.

When the Barbarians spotted these topsy-turvy weaklings, their general burst out laughing, "Hahahaha! I thought Mulan's soldiers are the best, but look at these! I don't have to lift a sword—or even a finger—to win this battle! What a piece of almond cake!"

The enemy soldiers roared with laughter, their armor sparkling under the northern sun while their spittle sprayed in all directions.

Thinking they had already won, the Barbarians let their guard down and fought only half-heartedly. All they thought was, "Hmmm... when will I finish my job so I can go home and enjoy my wife's delicious cooking?"

Just when the enemy was feeling relaxed, Mulan's best soldiers attacked from all sides. In a flash, they won the battle and chased the Barbarians out of China. All Mulan had to do was raise one finger to give the attack signal to her troops!

Because of this glorious victory, the emperor granted Mulan her wish to return home to her parents.

Back home, the villagers held a big celebration to welcome the invincible general. Everyone gathered around Mulan to pour out praise and gratitude. But Mulan went straight to her room to change. When she came back out in her woman's clothes, with hair piled up and smelling of fragrant jasmine, the villagers saw to their amazement that the famous warrior was in fact their neighbor girl.

One woman lovingly touched Mulan's sleeve. "Mulan, your bravery saved our country and its people's lives!

A little girl cried "When I grow up, I'll join the army, like you, and fight the Barbarians!"

A group of young men put their fists together in greeting and said, "Mulan, will you be our honorable teacher and pass your invincible kungfu to us?"

Han Shiqi couldn't take his eyes off the woman who was so strange, yet so familiar. "How can it be that I never noticed you were my future wife!"

For the first time in twelve years, Mulan blushed. The villagers clapped and cheered. Then they chopped vegetables and meat and lit the fires to cook the celebration feast.

Although Mulan was thought to have lived in China over a thousand years ago, we can still learn from her many noble qualities—her care for her parents; her bravery and courage in battle; her outstanding leadership; and her patriotism. Mulan has been a role model for girls, especially in traditional China where women were expected to stay home to look after the household. In modern China, women can accomplish anything they want, just like Mulan.

The Little Kungfu Warriors

Lingling loves the Mulan story. "Grandma," she begs, "please teach me kungfu so I can be a police officer when I grow up!"

Grandma lovingly kisses Lingling's cheeks, which are glowing like peaches. "Lingling, you can be whatever you want to if you study hard, work hard, and play hard. But I'm not sure I can teach you kungfu."

Lingling feels disappointed. "Why not?"

"Your great grand-pa taught me, and I learned a lot from him," replies Grandma, "but that was long ago. At my age, you expect me to do somersaults?"

"But, Grandma, please!" the children beg. "You're the best, always!"

The children keep on pleading and pulling at Grandma's apron. "All right," Grandma laughs. She disappears from the room and comes back with two little outfits. After the children put them on, Grandma Panda looks admiringly at her two little treasures. "Wah, you look like little warriors ready to fight! Come to the backyard and show me your kungfu!"

Surrounded by green plants and pink blossoms, Baobao stikes the "Panther Dashing into the Forest" pose.

Lingling stretches into a horse stance and performs "Bend the Bow and Shoot the Eagle."

Grandma Panda is very proud of her grandchildren. "Where did you learn all these movements?"

"Kungfu movies!" brother and sister shout.

Grandma laughs. "Good. Now watch me!"

Grandma Panda stands like a horse, her feet rooted on the ground like an ancient tree. She breathes long and deep like a hundred-year-old turtle, circulating her energy and pushing the air with her hands. Suddenly she jumps high and, with a swishing sound and a loud thud, lands with legs spread out in the Chinese character that means "one".

"Wah!" The little ones yell and clap till their palms turn pink.

In no time Grandma Panda springs up, then somersaults as if she were as light as a bouncing ping-pong ball.

"All right," Grandma says. "Enough of my kungfu. Now I'll teach you some." Soon the little pandas are kicking, jumping, spinning, somersaulting and shouting. But before too long their eyelids begin to droop. Grandma Panda puts an arm around each and leads them inside. No sooner are they tucked in bed than they fall fast asleep.

For health and self-defense, Chinese invented exercises to strengthen their bodies. They did this by imitating animals' movements and poses, such as the Praying Mantis and White Crane. Martial artists must also learn to breathe long and deep to help them draw upon their inner strength.

The Painted Faces of Chinese Opera

An hour later Baobao and Lingling are wide awake again. "Grandma, our tummies are rumbling like two angry dragons!"

Laughing, Grandma Panda brings them plates of steaming noodle soup. As they eat, their Grandma says, "This afternoon I am going to show you how to paint your faces so you look like Chinese opera heroes."

Lingling swallows a shrimp dumpling. "You mean like makeup?"

"No, Lingling, this is something different. In Chinese opera the actors' faces are painted so the audience will know who they are in the story." Grandma takes out some pictures and shows them to the children. "Look at these faces. See, this white face means he is an ordinary person, or a clown who's funny and won't hurt anyone."

Baobao picks up a piece of bright green broccoli. "What about green?"

Grandma smiles. "Ah, green-watch out! A green face means the person is cunning and cranky, so stay away from him."

"And black?" Baobao asks, now dipping the broccoli in a plate of black bean sauce.

"Black represents a righteous person—so respect him."

"What about red?" Lingling asks, popping a tomato into her mouth.

"Red is brave and courageous, like Mulan."

Lingling says, "Then I want my face painted red!"

"Grandma, what about gold? I want you to paint my face gold!" demands Baobao.

"Gold is either a nobleman or high official, so try to be like him."

Baobao casts Lingling a proud look. "I'm noble so you'd better learn from me."

Lingling retorts, "I'm brave, so you should…"

"All right, all right," interrupts Grandma, "you are both brave and noble. Anything else?"

In China, an opera is a play that uses singing, dancing, costumes and painted faces to help tell a story. Many Chinese opera stories are about virtues like goodness, loyalty, respect and courage. Chinese opera has been performed for thousands of years. Even children perform in Chinese opera!

Fun with Chinese Kites

The next morning is beautiful, with a clear bright sky—a perfect day to fly kites. In the park people are scattered all around. Some are practicing kungfu, and some are strolling around or relaxing on benches, enjoying the good weather. Grandma sits under an ancient tree and takes three colorful kites from her big tote bag. "You know how to fly these?" she asks. The children nod. "Good." Grandma Panda holds up kites in the shape of a scorpion, a butterfly, and a goldfish. "Lingling, which one do you want?" "The butterfly." "Baobao?" "Scorpion, of course!" "OK, then I get the goldfish." As she gives the children their kites, Grandma tells them the story of how kites were invented.

Once upon a time there lived a talented inventor called Luban who loved to make things with his large, skillful hands. One day as he sat in his house thinking up new inventions, a bird outside his window caught his attention. Watching the bird soar in the air, he decided to make a wooden bird that could fly just like the real one.

Alas, three years passed and, though Luban tried many different mechanical devices, the bird refused to fly. Frustrated, the inventor jumped on the bird's back and kicked hard. "You stupid wooden bird! Why won't you take me for a ride in the sky?"

Just then, to Luban's utter surprise, the creature made a loud "Quuuiiiii, Quuuiiiii" sound, flapped its wings, lifted off the ground with Luban on top, and flew outside, screaming "Quuueeek! Quuueeek! Quuueeek!" "Wah! I made it! I made it! I can't believe I'm that good!" Luban laughed and laughed.

The bird kept flapping its wooden wings while Luban enjoyed the scenery below—mountains, houses that were like tiny toys, the wide sea as blue as his silk gown, boats floating like curled-up leaves. The wooden bird flew on and on. Finally, it flew back to Luban's house, where it crashed into his flower garden!

26

Luban's uncle saw all this from his room. So one day after Luban went out, the uncle flew the bird to the neighboring village, expecting a huge, heroic welcome. But when the villagers rushed out to look at this strange sight, instead of praising the old man's magical power, they pointed to him, screaming, "Monster! Get rid of this unlucky monster!"

The old man screamed back, "Wait, brothers and sisters, I'm no monster, and this bird is just a toy invented by my nephew!" Before anyone could answer, a strong wind blew from nowhere and knocked both old man and bird down to the ground."

Aii—ya!" Old Man rubbed his sore bottom. "Villagers, now can you see I'm no monster, but just an ordinary old man?"

One mother cried, "Please, people, don't believe him! All monsters are able to transform themselves into whatever they want." A group of young men shook their fists. "Let's get rid of him! Now!"

All the villagers rushed to the old man and smashed the wooden bird. Sadly, no one else ever learned the secret of making wooden birds that fly. But centuries later, people discovered that by using paper they could make kites that soared just as high as Luban's wooden bird. Everyone remembered Luban as the inventor of the first kite.

"The Chinese people of long ago used kites to deliver mail and send messages to their ancestors, but now we fly kites for fun" Grandma says. "They come in lots of different colors and shapes, like bats, phoenixes, dragons—even the Moon Goddess and the Monkey King.

"Wow!" Baobao exclaims. "I want the Monkey King!"

"And I want the Moon Goddess!" Lingling cries.

Grandma Panda laughs. "Baobao and Lingling, why don't you fly your scorpion and butterfly first?"

"Yes!" the children shout, dashing off to lift up their kites!

Grandma Panda Sings an Old Farewell Song

And then one day, summer in Grandma Panda's cozy, happy home is over and it's time to say good-bye.

With Grandma's help, the two children sadly pack their bags and lunch boxes for the long ride home.

Her mouth turned down like a capsized boat, Lingling whines, "Grandma, I don't want to go home!"

"Neither do I!" cries Baobao. "I want to fly more kites. And do more kungfu. And paint more Chinese characters. And hear more stories and eat more dim sum! And... let us stay, please!"

Grandma Panda pats their heads, which are round as two basketballs. "I'd love you to stay too. But you have to go back to school. Besides, your mommy and daddy want you back. They miss you, and you miss them too."

"But Grandma, we learn so much from you!" Lingling cries.

"Okay, before you leave I'll teach you one more thing—the most popular Chinese farewell song." Grandma Panda dashes to her room and comes back out with a long wooden object.

Eyes sparkling with curiosity, Baobao studies the object with seven strings mounted across its long body. "Grandma, what's this?"

"The qin, a musical instrument older than your Mommy, Daddy, and me added together."

"Grandma, are you going to teach us how to play the qin now?" Lingling asks hopefully.

"We don't have time now, Lingling," Grandma replies, "but I'll play the qin and sing you a very old farewell song called 'Three Variations On the Yang Pass'."

Grandma sings...

In Wei City the morning rain washes the dust away

The guest house is green like the swaying willow

My friend, please have one more cup of tea

Beyond the Yang Pass, you will be traveling alone.

When the song is over, it is time to say goodbye.

Grandma Panda checks her grandchildren's backpacks one more time, and walks with them down the road toward the waiting bus.

"Good-bye, Grandma! We'll miss you!" the children cry.

"I'll miss you too. But you'll come again soon, won't you?" Grandma Panda asks, her eyes misty as she hugs and kisses them goodbye.

"Grandma, please don't cry. We'll come again soon!" Baobao and Lingling call as they scamper toward the bus, turning once more to wave good-bye while their Grandma softly hums "Three Variations on the Yang Pass."

"Three Variations On The Yang Pass" is a very old poem that was set to music hundreds of years ago. "Three variations" means three different ways of playing the same melody. The qin is the oldest string instrument in China. It has been played in small gatherings of friends who may also paint, recite poetry, do calligraphy, drink tea, and appreciate snow and flowers together.

Published by Tuttle Publishing, an imprint of Periplus Editions (HK) Ltd.

www.tuttlepublishing.com

Library of Congress Cataloging-in-Publication Data in progress

ISBN 978-0-8048-4149-8

Distributed by

North America, Latin America & Europe
Tuttle Publishing, 364 Innovation Drive,
North Clarendon, VT 05759-9436 U.S.A.
Tel: 1 (802) 773-8930; Fax: 1 (802) 773-6993
info@tuttlepublishing.com; www.tuttlepublishing.com

Japan
Tuttle Publishing, Yaekari Building, 3rd Floor,
5-4-12 Osaki, Shinagawa-ku, Tokyo 141 0032
Tel: (81) 3 5437-0171; Fax: (81) 3 5437-0755
sales@tuttle.co.jp; www.tuttle.co.jp

Asia Pacific
Berkeley Books Pte. Ltd., 61 Tai Seng Avenue
#02-12, Singapore 534167
Tel: (65) 6280-1330; Fax: (65) 6280-6290
inquiries@periplus.com.sg; www.periplus.com

Indonesia
PT Java Books Indonesia,
Kawasan Industri Pulogadung
Jl. Rawa Gelam IV No. 9, Jakarta 13930, Indonesia
Tel: 62 (21) 4682-1088; Fax: (62) 21 461-0206
crm@periplus.co.id; www.periplus.com

First edition

17 16 15 14 13   10 9 8 7 6 5 4 3 2 1

EP1301

Printed in Malaysia

TUTTLE PUBLISHING® is a registered trademark of Tuttle Publishing, a division of Periplus Editions (HK) Ltd.

The Tuttle Story: "Books to Span the East and West"

Most people are surprised to learn that the world's largest publisher of books on Asia had its humble beginnings in the tiny American state of Vermont. The company's founder, Charles E. Tuttle, belonged to a New England family steeped in publishing. And his first love was naturally books—especially old and rare editions.

Immediately after WW II, serving in Tokyo under General Douglas MacArthur, Tuttle was tasked with reviving the Japanese publishing industry. He later founded the Charles E. Tuttle Publishing Company, which thrives today as one of the world's leading independent publishers.

Though a westerner, Tuttle was hugely instrumental in bringing a knowledge of Japan and Asia to a world hungry for information about the East. By the time of his death in 1993, Tuttle had published over 6,000 books on Asian culture, history and art—a legacy honored by the Japanese emperor with the "Order of the Sacred Treasure," the highest tribute Japan can bestow upon a non-Japanese.

With a backlist of 1,500 titles, Tuttle Publishing is more active today than at any time in its past—inspired by Charles Tuttle's core mission to publish fine books to span the East and West and provide a greater understanding of each.